DARKNESS
SLIPPED IN

For my friends and family,
and thanks to Steve, Mike, and the AHRC

Distributed in Canada by H. B. Fenn and Company Ltd.

Library of Congress Cataloging-in-Publication Data
has been applied for.

ISBN: 978-0-7534-6209-6

Kingfisher books are available for special promotions and premiums.
For details contact: Director of Special Markets, Holtzbrinck Publishers.

First American Edition June 2008
Printed in India
2 4 6 8 10 9 7 5 3 1
1TR/0108/THOM/SCHOY(SCHOY)/157MA/C

Darkness
Slipped In

Ella Burfoot

KINGFISHER
NEW YORK

Daisy was thinking of a game to play

when Darkness slipped in at the end of the day.

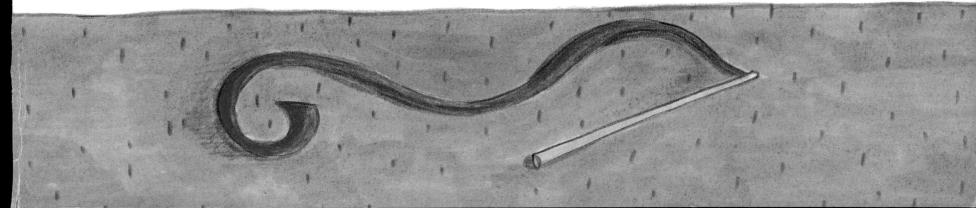

He came in through the window
and spread out on the floor.

While Daisy danced and laughed and played—
then danced around some more.

Pretending that he wasn't there,
he slid along the wall.

But Daisy had seen Darkness,
and she wasn't scared at all.

He quickly filled the room
and ate up all the light.

But Daisy knew
that Darkness knew

she had him in her sight.

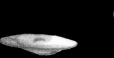

With one swift move
she crossed the room
and grabbed him by the wrist.

And pretty soon,
around the room

they danced the FUNKY TWIST!

And after all that dancing around,
they had a little break.

They sipped a cup of lemonade
and nibbled on some cake.

Now Darkness comes
in every night

to dance and laugh and play.

And the two of them, the best of friends, dance the night away.

But when they're tired and sleepy,
Daisy switches off the light.
And Daisy knows
that Darkness knows
it's time to say . . .

"Good night."